HIGH WINDS

SYLVAN OSWALD

JESSICA FLEISCHMANN

PRELUDE

A TISSUE-BOX
APARTMENT
WITHOUT
A VIEW OF
ANYTHING.

HIGH WINDS LIES IN BED
COVERED IN MEN'S MAGAZINES.
BOLD-SMELLING BLOOM IN
THE AIR.

STOPS WAITING FOR SLEEP AT 5 A.M.

GETS MAD AT ART. WRITES INSIDE HIS BOOKS.

CLIMBS OUT WINDOW. SCRATCHES FACE
ON NEIGHBOR'S FRUIT TREES. BORROWS
NEIGHBOR'S OLD BLACK TRUCK WITHOUT
ASKING. TURNS UP FAIRFAX INTO THE HILLS.

DRIVES THROUGH VINTAGE POSTCARDS
TO FIND HIS HALF BROTHER.

NOT A STORY OF LOSS BUT OF NEGLECT.
AND OF INVENTION. AND WHAT WAS

INVENTED WAS NOT VERY NICE. AND HE
THINKS HE DIDN'T DO ANYTHING

DOESN'T EVEN KNOW WHAT HE DID.

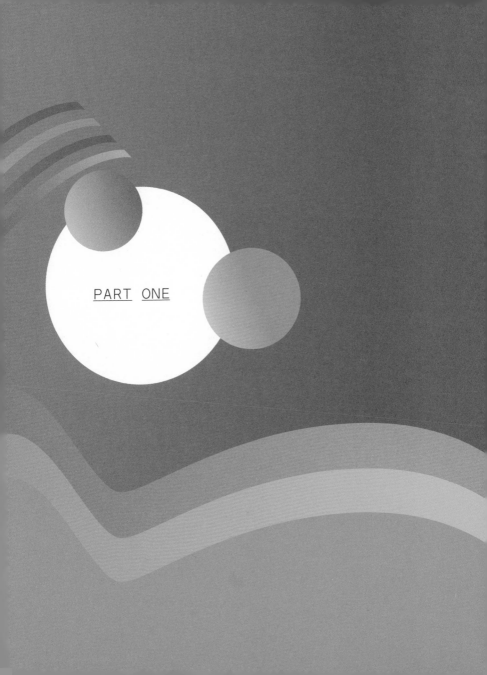

PART ONE

BACKUP SINGERS. HANDCLAPS. THE OCCASIONAL FALSE RHYME.

HIGH WINDS BLASTS OUT OF THE CITY AND SHOOTS

TOWARDS SOME IDEA OF THE DESERT.

SHOOTING BEING FULL OF FANTASY

ESPECIALLY IF WE'RE ALL RIDING HORSES

OR IMAGINING THAT SUCH A THING IS POSSIBLE.

TEENAGE HORSEBACK GANG IN OUR 1995 CLOTHING.

DO WE DEFEND OUR TOWN?

DISCUSSION.

HIGH WINDS TUCKS HIS COCK INTO HIS PANTS
AND IT'S A WESTERN.

NOW EVERYBODY TRY.

2

SEXY
BEFORE HE
KNEW WHAT
THAT WAS —

IN THE SAME CLOTHES
FOR DAYS LIKE HIS
DRIFTER FANTASY.

TOBACCO-BROWN LEATHER SHIRT CLINGS TO A BLOND MOVIE COWBOY. MOLDED TO HIS BODY BY SWEAT AND RIDING.

HIS HALF BROTHER BANTAM IS
ON TO BEER SMELLS AND
BROKEN GUITAR STRINGS.

COWBOYS DON'T LIVE WITH
THEIR PARENTS
HE SNARLS.

SO?

CAN'T
STAY HERE
ANYMORE.

PARENTS BEING A LOOSE TERM
TO DESCRIBE THEIR FATHER
HERE
AND THEIR MOTHER
THERE.

WHERE ARE
YOU GOING?

MY APARTMENT.

FOREIGN TERM.

HOW DO YOU
GET THERE?

VINTAGE
TOYOTA CELICA.

WHAT ABOUT ME?

YOU DON'T HAVE AN
APARTMENT.

BANTAM THROWS ALL HIS
ROCK BAND T-SHIRTS IN
THE BACK SEAT.

WHAT KIND OF NAME
IS BANTAM! HIGH WINDS
SHOUTS AFTER HIM.

NEVER USED TO PUFF HIS
CHEST. KNOWS THAT HE
CAN'T BACK IT UP.

LITTLE HIGH WINDS TALKS TOUGH!

YOU'RE TOO OLD TO BE A RUNAWAY.

SWINGING AT ARM'S LENGTH.

I'M NOT. BANTAM PUTS IT
IN REVERSE. YOU CAN
HAVE MY PORN.

AND LEAVES HIGH WINDS
AT AGE ELEVEN WITH
LONG HAIR AND PROTO
QUEER WHO STILL
THINKS PASTA IS GOOD
FOR HIM.

WILL ONE DAY BE HORRIFIED
TO LEARN HIS PROFESSIONAL
OBLIGATION TO PRETEND
EVERYTHING IS EXCITING.

EASY ACCESS TO
DOOM.

BUT ON THE BRIGHT
SIDE NOBODY CARES.

3

OLDEST GAS STATION IN THE WORLD. BOY
APPEARS AND OFFERS TO WORK THE PUMP.
WHY NOT. HIGH WINDS DUCKS INSIDE THE
SHOP TO DISCOVER THAT WORLD'S OLDEST

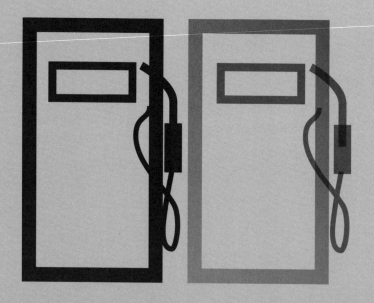

GAS STATION STOCKS WORLD'S OLDEST
MAGAZINES. LOUSY WITH TOM SELLECK.
ALL HIS DREAMS OF JUST ENOUGH FUZZ
TO CAMOUFLAGE HIS SCARS.

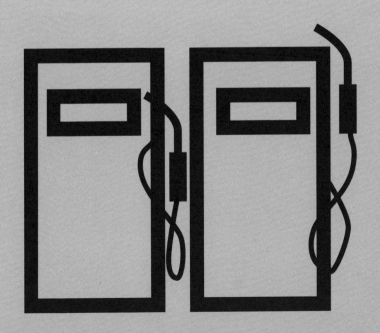

SUDDENLY BUSTLING. DUDES IN THE
STALLS. ALL FULL. WEIGHS OPTIONS.
DECIDES TO WAIT.

BOY STILL PUMPING. EYES SCAN RAGS: MEN
WITH GUNS, MEN WITH SURFBOARDS, MEN ON
HORSES, MEN IN CARS. IDEAS OF MEN AND
IS HE ONE OF THEM. SOME PEOPLE THINK SO.
BUT WHAT DOES HE THINK.

JUST KNOWS HE'S NOT LIKE THEM.

REMEMBERS THE TIME A FRIEND OF
A FRIEND CAME BY TO PICK UP
VEGETABLES. THE TIME A PORN
COULD HAVE ACTUALLY HAPPENED.
THEY DIDN'T KNOW EACH OTHER.
CORDIAL BUT HOLDING BREATH.
SHORT WORDS. SWEATY PALMS. SOOO
NICE TO MEET YOU.

THROWS TOM SELLECK ON THE
PASSENGER SEAT AND SPEEDS OFF.

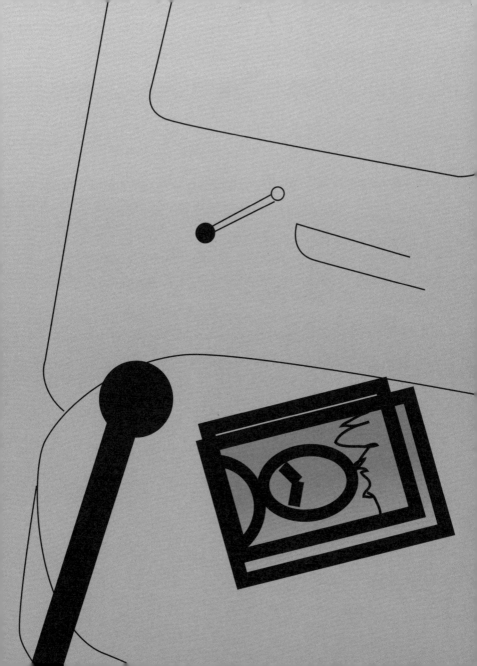

4

CAN'T SLEEP FOR A REASON. MANIC
PTERODACTYL IN BRAIN HAS ENDLESS
LIST OF GRIEVANCES REQUIRING
IMMEDIATE ATTENTION. RAMPED BY EVERY
DROOP OF EYELID.

JUST TRY AND VANQUISH.

THE CREATURE HAS NO PATIENCE.
THE CREATURE NEEDS TO FEED.

EVERY DAY WAS UNABRIDGED.
PARTS THAT SHOULD HAVE BEEN
DELETED DARK OR NEVER KNOWN.

NO HELP FROM SEX DRUGS BOOKS
RUNS HERBS OR RHYTHMIC BREATHING.
HIGH WINDS TRIED EVERYTHING.

BECAME AN EXPERT ON NAT-U-RAL
REMEDIES. IF YOU WANT TO KNOW
MORE

HE'S
YOUR
GUY.

SEE APPENDIX.

DOESN'T KNOW HOW TO HAVE A BROTHER
LET ALONE HALF.

TRY NOT TO FEEL ANYTHING ABOUT HIM.

WOULD MAKE MORE SENSE IF

THEY SPUTTERED OR DROOLED

THEY WON OR LOST OR TIED

THEY FOUGHT WITH WORDS OR

SHED SOME BLOOD IN THE DIRT.

PART TWO

HIGH WINDS GETS TO NEW MEXICO
IN ABOUT TEN MINUTES.

LIKE MAD MAGAZINE   FOLD-INS.

FOLD OUT

LIKE MID-1950S

ACCORDION

POSTCARDS.

WONDERFUL

CARLSBAD

FOUND AT STORE
THAT ALSO SELLS

CRYSTALS

CAVERNS

NEW MEXICO.

TAXIDERMY AND

SMALL ANIMAL
SKELETONS.

BRIEF HISTORY.

ACTUAL COWBOY OF SIXTEEN "DISCOVERS" BLACKEST
HOLE BY TRACKING CLOUD OF BATS
TO THEIR CAVE.

1901.

FASHIONS APPARATUS FOR LOWERING BODY
INTO EARTH. METHOD ONE: WIRE LADDER.
METHOD TWO: GUANO BUCKET.

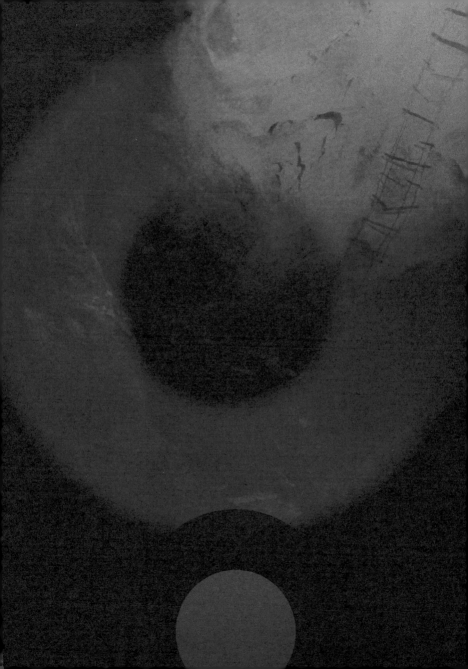

EYES WEEKS FEET LANTERN TILL
HE'S ALMOST MAPPED IT.

HE NAMES EACH ONE EACH

TEENAGE LANDFORM

BONEYARD
BOTTOMLESS PIT
WHALE'S MOUTH
FAIRYLAND
LAKE OF THE CLOUDS

AND SOME OTHER NOW OFFENSIVE
NAMES.
SEE IF YOU CAN LOCATE THEM ALL.

SEE MAP.

THEN THE GOVERNMENT STEPPED IN.

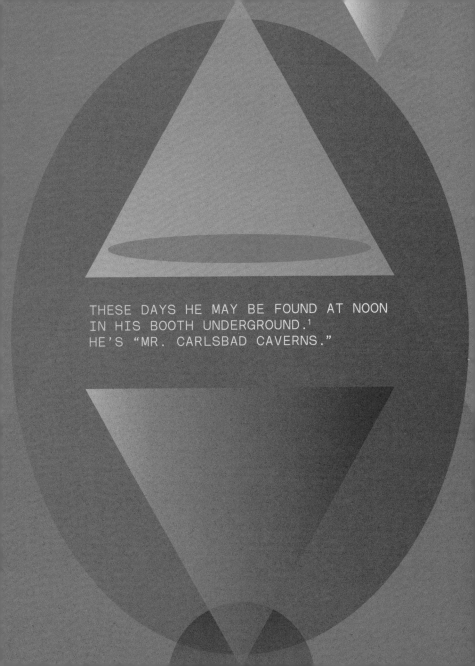

THESE DAYS HE MAY BE FOUND AT NOON
IN HIS BOOTH UNDERGROUND.[1]
HE'S "MR. CARLSBAD CAVERNS."

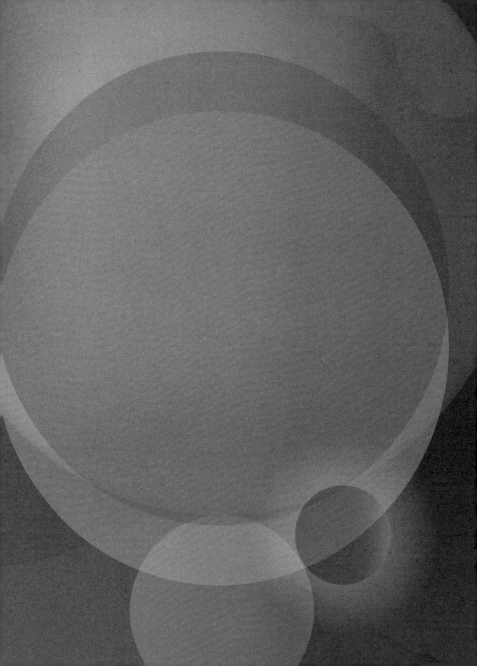

7

COLD PULL OF THE SOARING
BOTTOMLESS THEATER.

THE CAVERNS' NATURAL ENTRANCE.

SO THIS IS A GAPING MAW.

EARTH'S PRIVATE PLACE

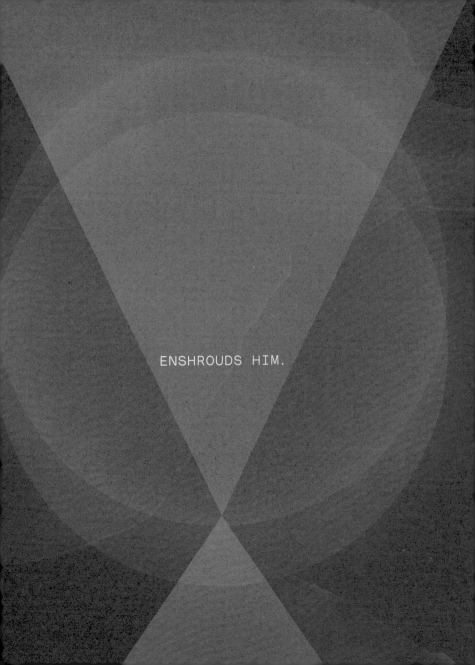

ENSHROUDS HIM.

WE LIVE ON A PLANET.

CAVE SWALLOWS FLY ALMOST ECSTATIC CIRCLES.

HIGH WINDS CHARGES DOWN THE DIMLY LIT PATH INTO ROCOCO EMPTINESS.

FAMILY PHOTO OPS
SQUEEZE AND
RELEASE HIM.

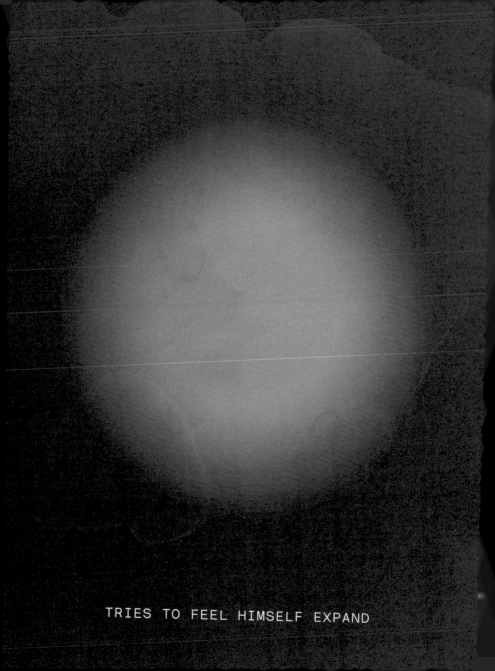

TRIES TO FEEL HIMSELF EXPAND

BETWEEN PULSES.

8

SIGHT OF
HIS
BROTHER'S
GUITARS...

DID HE EVER GIVE BACK THE ONE HE BORROWED...

SIGHT AND SMELL
OF BANTAM'S
DISASTROUS
ROOM. MESS
BEYOND
COMPREHENSION..

TAKING OVER THE ROOM AFTER HE LEFT.

FINDING EVEN MORE PORN...

COMPLAINT ABOUT THE CEREAL...

CARVING BANTAM'S INITIALS INTO THE PIANO STARTED WITH LEANING TOO HARD ON THE PINK FLAMINGO PEN FROM MCDONALD'S HAPPY MEAL, AND THEN TRYING TO MAKE IT SEEM LIKE NOTHING HAPPENED. FAILED ATTEMPT TO MAKE IT SEEM LIKE WHAT CAN'T REMEMBER. NO GOOD EXPLANATION. FOG. 'TEMPORARY INSANITY' OR SOME SHIT. CUT TURNED INTO LINE TURNED INTO CURVE TURNED INTO INITIALS. SORT OF LIKE OH THIS WOULD BE BAD OH THIS IS HAPPENING. OH. OH. MAYBE NO ONE WILL NOTICE.

BACK SEAT OF HIS TWO-DOOR
CAR... OLIVE GREEN AND SMALL...
WHAT WAS IT.
LITTLE TEARDROP-SHAPED
WINDOW. MOTION SICK.

QUIZ ON NAMES OF ROLLING STONES.

SIGHT OF THAT FIRST APARTMENT AROUND THE CORNER.

PHOTOGRAPH.
CLOUDY PARKING LOT.
BANTAM'S SKINNY LEGS.
HIGH WINDS' CHUBBY
BABY BODY.
BURGER KING CROWN.

9

EACH DAY IS THE SAME UNDERGROUND.
56 DEGREES.

JUST ASK EMPLOYEES OF THE CARLSBAD
CAVERNS LUNCH ROOM CAFETERIA.

THEY DON'T SEE THE SUN.

THEY DEADPAN STRIPTEASE
STANDARD-ISSUE FLEECE.
REVEAL OLD-TIMEY
SODA JERK OUTFITS.

THEY SING:

WHAT DO YOU DO WHEN
THERE'S SOMETHING
YOU CRAVE
BUT YOU'RE NINE HUNDRED
FEET BELOW GROUND
IN A CAVE?

YOU'D GIVE YOUR LEFT BALL
FOR A PLATE OF FRENCH
FRIES:
CHOLESTEROL NOW! OR ELSE
SOMEBODY DIES!

THE GOOD NEWS, MY
FRIENDS, IS YOU'RE NOT
IN SIBERIA!
YOU'RE AT CARLSBAD
CAVERNS LUNCH ROOM
CAFETERIA!

YOU THOUGHT THAT A LITTLE
BEEF JERKY WOULD HOLD YA.
WE'RE SORRY THERE'S NO
OUTSIDE FOOD, HATE TO
SCOLD YA.

THEN MOTHER-IN-LAW FOUND
YOU DOWN ON YOUR KNEES.
NO NOTHING LIKE THAT,
YOU JUST WANTED
GRILLED CHEESE!

WE KNOW WHAT YOU WEARY
SPELUNKERS NEED
AFTER YOUR COFFEE YOUR
METH AND YOUR WEED!

THE GOOD NEWS, MY
FRIENDS, IS YOU'RE NOT
IN SIBERIA!
THIS IS CARLSBAD CAVERNS
LUNCH ROOM CAFETERIA!

[GRAND FINALE]
WHO'S GOT THE SUGAR AND
FAT THAT'LL CHEER YA?
WHO'S GOT THE SNACKS
THAT'LL MEET YOUR
CRITERYA?
WHO'S GOT A CLEAN BILL
OF HEALTH — NO LISTERYA!
CARLSBAD CAVERNS
LUNCH ROOM CAFETERIA!

(WE DON'T SERVE DINNER,
HONEY.)
CARLSBAD CAVERNS
LUNCH ROOM CAFETERIA!

[MOVIE MUSICAL: TRY TO REPLICATE
THE LOOK OF THE ACTUAL CARLSBAD
CAVERNS LUNCH ROOM FROM THE 1950S,
LIKE AN AUTOMAT INSIDE A MOUNTAIN.
COUNTERS AND FIXTURES LIGHT WHAT'S
BELOW THEM LIKE UFOS. THEY SEEM
TO HOVER. BUT EVERYTHING ABOVE
IS STILL SUPER DARK BECAUSE IT'S
A CAVE. MORE CONVEYOR BELTS THAN
NECESSARY TRACK ALONG BEARING
ALL-AMERICAN FAST FOOD. CLOSE-UP:
THE PLATES ROTATE AS THEY CONVEY.
THE GREASY FOOD WINKS A DISNEY
SPARKLE. TOURIST-PATRONS CARRY TRAYS
WITH FOOD AND DRINK. DANCE TOSSING
TRAYS IN AIR. FOOD STAYS PUT.

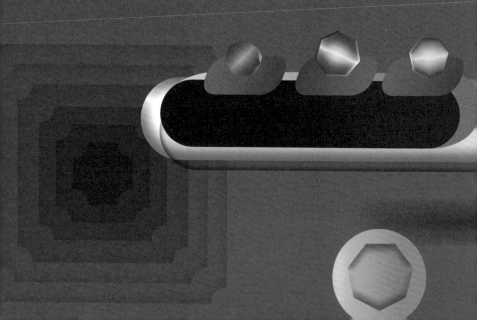

SPELUNKERS IN HELMETS WITH LIGHTS
SWING IN FROM THE CEILING. A
HANGRY PARENT SPANKING A CHILD
SIPS A SUGARY DRINK FROM A STRAW.
IMMEDIATELY STOPS SPANKING AND
BECOMES DELIGHTEDLY BLOATED. KID,
STILL OVER KNEE, LOOKS BACK IN
CONFUSION. MANY LITTLE BATS FLY
IN FROM ABOVE IN THE GRAND FINALE
ADDING THEIR SCREECHY HARMONY TO
THE TAG LINE IN SUCH GREAT NUMBERS
THAT THEY BLOT OUT THE SCENE AND
TAKE US INTO... BLACKOUT.]

HIGH WINDS LIGHTS A CIGARETTE.

SPIRITUALLY.

10

EATS A MEAL OF HOT DOGS AND CANDY.

DEEP INSIDE AMERICA.

CUT.

ENTER CARLSBAD CAVERNS POSTAL WORKER
UNWITTINGLY SULTRY WITH PURPOSE.

POSTCARD FOR HIGH WINDS.

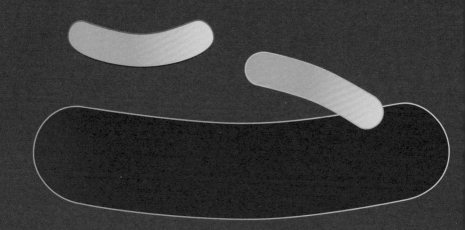

HIGH WINDS AGE 6 CURLED UP IN BOARD GAME
CLOSET OFFICE.

RACQUET BALLS AND EXTRA DINING-TABLE
LEAVES

FORTRESS OF AMAZING THOUGHTS

PALACE OF EFFORTLESSNESS

(DINOSAUR DAYS)

AND FAMILY ARCHIVE.

CIGAR BOXES MATCHBOOKS AND POSTCARDS
FROM PEOPLE WHO DON'T EXIST ANYMORE

PASSED DOWN THROUGH MEN.

GREAT-GRANDFATHER'S TRIP TO LAKE COMO
PROBABLY ONLY TRIP IN HIS LIFE DID HE
FIGHT IN A WAR CAN'T REMEMBER.

CAN'T REMEMBER CAN'T REMEMBER

AND POSTCARDS BETRAY NOTHING.

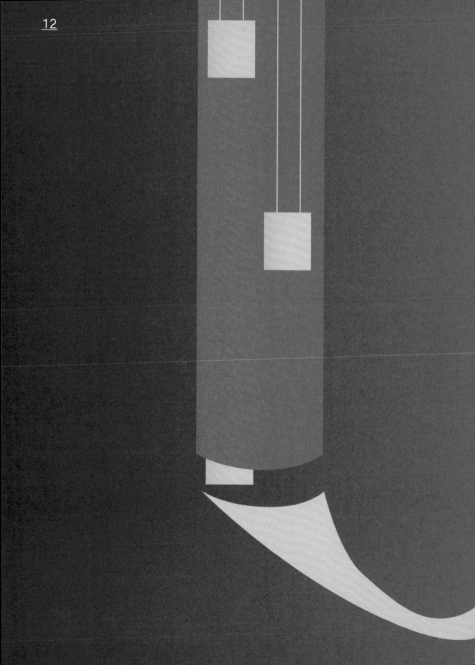

YEAR OF HIS BIRTH
A MOST ABSURD SCENE.[2]

FOUR MEN RIDE
ELEVATOR DOWN
INTO CAVERNS.

APPROACH UNDERGROUND
INFORMATION DESK
AKA "UGLY DESK."

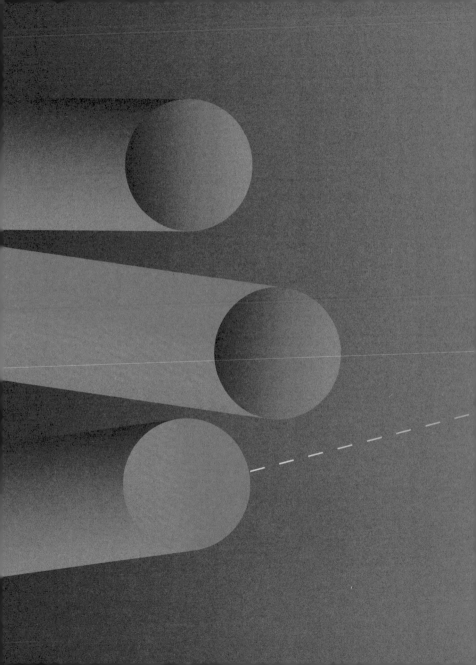

PULL GUNS. GET ON PA. ANNOUNCE HOLDUP.

THIS IS FOR REAL. WARNING SHOT.

PEOPLE WEIRDLY NOT THAT CONCERNED.
1979.

TAKE LINDA HOSTAGE. DEMAND A MILLION
DOLLARS. DEMAND AIRPLANE TO BRAZIL.
EAT LUNCH.

OFFER TO PAY. GET ARRESTED.

DIDN'T CONSIDER: TRAPPED IN CAVE.

13

DEAR HIGH WINDS

NO ONE IS WATCHING YOU.

POSTMARK:
WHITE
SANDS

HANG TIGHT STALACTITES.

PART THREE

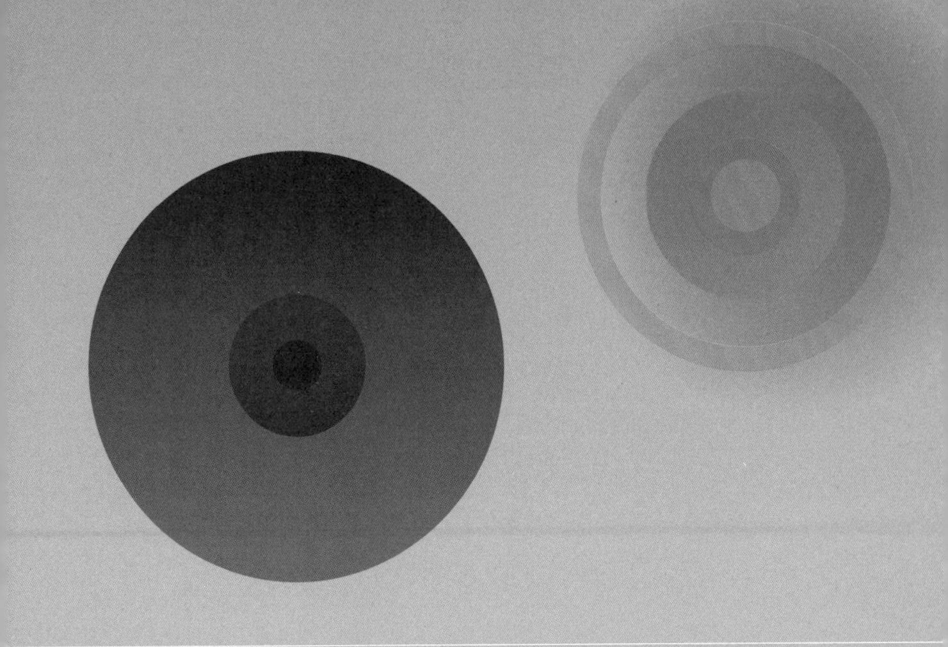

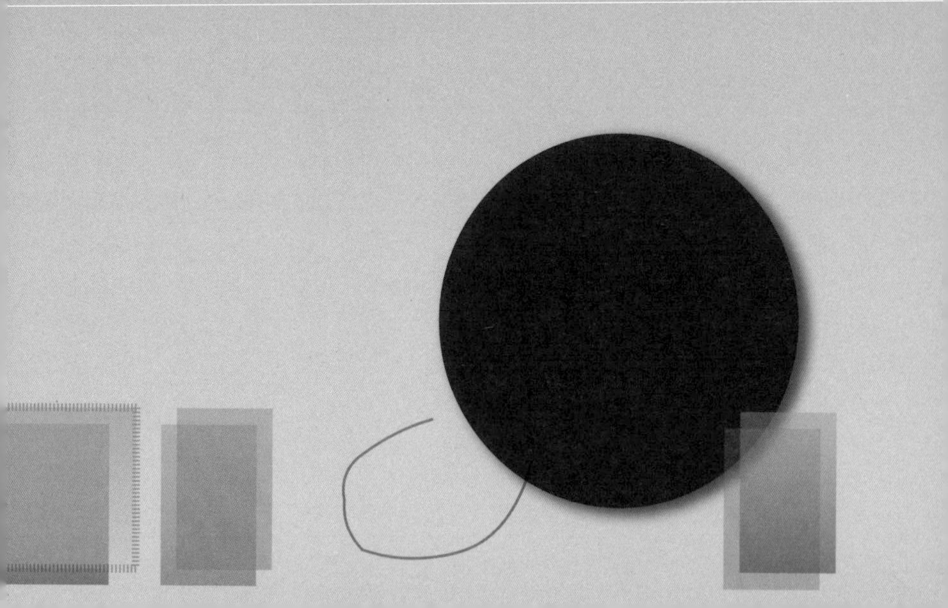

14

DRIVES IN SOME KIND OF STATE.

THIS YEAR WAS BETTER NUMB.
AESTHETIC CRISIS VERSUS
MAYBE JUST BUSTED.

ALL BOOKS TOO WORDS

ALL INTERNET TOO PANIC

ALL ART TOO BUSINESS

ALL THOUGHTS BEEN DONE

SPILLED TEA ON PILE OF CUE-CARD
AFFIRMATIONS.

NEW RULE STOP CLEANING!

NEW RULE STOP CARING!

DO NOT REPEAT DO NOT CLARIFY MAGIC!

CRASHED HIS CAR SO EMBARRASSING
AND DESTROYED ALL PLAYS.

MIGHT BE TOO LATE TO LEARN
ABOUT POETRY.

PHONE BOOTH OUTSIDE WHITE SANDS GYPSUM DUNES
HAS ACTUAL PHONE BOOK IN IT

LEFT BEHIND BY ANCIENT SEA.

THEY SAY THESE DUNES KEEP MOVING.

WE THINK
SURE SAND BLOWS
SURE BEACHES ERODE
THAT'S NORMAL.

BUT FOR GREAT MASSES OF SAND TO MOVE
LIKE HOW MUCH DO THEY MOVE
THAT'S ONE SOUNDTRACK SHY OF A HORROR FLICK
TO SOMEONE INDOORSY.

OPENS PHONE BOOK.

SLIGHT VIBRATION FROM GROUND.
MAP SAYS MILITARY RANGE NOT FAR.
MISSILE PRACTICE.

WHAT IS THIS PLACE.

PHONE BOOK ADVERTISEMENT.
AMATEUR BOXERS NEED HELP REACHING
BANTAM WEIGHT? CALL TODAY AND
MENTION THIS AD FOR A DISCOUNT.

16

STALL TACTICS. TRUTH OR CONSEQUENCES
IS ACTUALLY THE NAME OF THIS TOWN.

NOT SURE WHAT HE NEEDS IN THIS STORE.

UNDERWEAR IN PACKAGE WHY SO APPEALING

ALL ONE NEEDS FOR GRILLING
AND EVERY INTENTION OF CAMPING.

RUBBERIZED WHATSITS

WATER WINGS FOR MOTEL POOLS

AND GUNS DON'T LOOK AT THE GUNS.

CASHIER ITCHES HIM WITH HER EYES.
WAIT WAS THAT A BUTCH NOD ('SUP).

MAYBE NOT.

BUY PRICKLY PEAR CACTUS CANDY
FOR PAY PHONE CHANGE.

USE SMALL WORDS OR NONE.

CLAW FOR WAY OUT OF JOURNEY.

BUT SHORT FINGERNAILS.

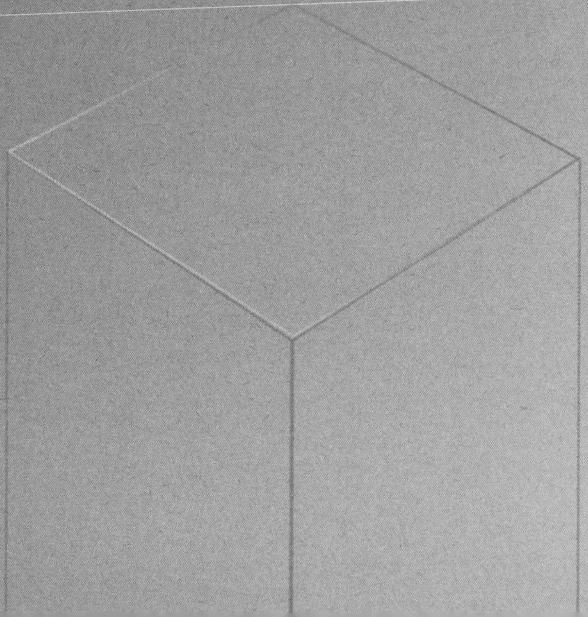

BEEP. HELLO. CLEARING MY THROAT. FIXING MY
PITCH. THIS IS HIGH WINDS. CALLING IN REFERENCE
TO YOUR AD. NOT SURE HOW OLD IT IS. COULDN'T
BELIEVE IT. PHONE BOOK AD. SO I CALLED.
I HOPE YOUR OFFER STILL STANDS.

PART FOUR

PRIVATE ROAD NO TRESPASSERS. WE DON'T CALL 911.

HIGH WINDS WHIPS NEIGHBOR'S TRUCK UP
LONG DIRT DRIVE.

SPLASHES OVER SHALLOW STREAMS LIKE
CAR COMMERCIAL.

WHOLE THING MORE HEROIC IF JUBILANT MINIVANS
FROM CAMP OUR SAVIOR WOULD LET HIM PASS.

SING-SONG THEIR TURNOFF FINALLY.

BUZZING OF INSECTS. OR RATTLESNAKES.

AFTER SHARP TURN COMES TO STOP
AND DUST CLOUD SETTLES.

PATCHWORK PLACE ALL SALVAGE. NO CARS PARKED.
BREEZE CARRIES FAINT TANG OF HALF BROTHER.
DID HE BUILD IT HIMSELF. COULD HAVE.
HASN'T BEEN BANTAM FOR YEARS.

HIGH WINDS WALKS AROUND SHAGGY HOUSE
PEERING INTO WINDOWS. DOG BOWL NO DOG.
HEAVY IRON LAMPS. PLAID BLANKET. AND
WHAT MAKES IT BANTAM'S: CLOTHES STREWN
ABOUT. ASHTRAYS OVERFLOWING. DISHES
IN SINK. WRENCHES NEXT TO DEAD PLANTS.
OLD BATHTUB ON BACK PORCH LITTERED
WITH EMPTIES.

SPIES DARK-WALLED BEDROOM. MIDNIGHT
SHEETS UNTUCKED. DUST NOT BOTHERED TO
DANCE IN SUNBEAM. PLACE YOU TAKE SOMEONE
TO FUCK AND THEN THEY LEAVE. SOFT FOCUS
OUT WINDOW WHILE YOU GO AT IT HARD
THINKING HOW YOU STILL DON'T KNOW NAMES
OF TREES. PLACE OF OBLIVION.

ALWAYS WANTING A ROOM LIKE THAT. CAN'T
BEAR MESS FOR LONG ENOUGH TO BUILD UP
DUNGEON ATMOSPHERE. YET DISCIPLINED
IN POINTLESS WAYS. LIKE DOING DISHES
IMMEDIATELY AFTER OVEREATING. LIKE
HOURS OF WRITING TAKEN OVER BY
PREPARING FOR GYM GOING TO GYM
RECOVERING FROM GYM. AGORAPHOBIA WITH
A FOUR-BLOCK RADIUS. CAN'T IMAGINE
TRAINERS IN REGULAR CLOTHES. WHAT DO
THEIR APARTMENTS LOOK LIKE. DO THEY
SOCIALIZE TOGETHER. ONE OF THEM SAID
HE HAD THE FRAME OF A MUAY THAI
FIGHTER AND TAUGHT HIM TO KICK AND
THROW PUNCHES BUT JUST AS EXERCISE AND
HE DREADS EVER DOING IT IN REAL LIFE.

BUT TESTOSTERONE QUICKENS ANGER AND
MAKES VIOLENCE FEEL POSSIBLE. MAKES
BODY PUBLIC. PEOPLE TOUCH HIS CHEST
FOR EMPHASIS. PRACTICES TAKING SHIRT
OFF AND NOT FEELING NAKED.

20

COULD BE PERCEIVED AS CREEPY RIGHT NOW.
SHOULD STOP PEERING.

FINDS KNIFE IN POCKET.

POSSIBLE SELF DEFENSE DEFENSE.

HE REALLY SHOULD GO.

BUT LOOK.

WILD ROSEMARY TO TIE WITH TWINE AND ADMIRE
AT BREAKFAST.

WANTS A SOUVENIR ABHORS A SHOWDOWN.

GET IT OR FORGET IT.

DO LOUIS L'AMOUR HEROES EXPLAIN THEIR NAMES?

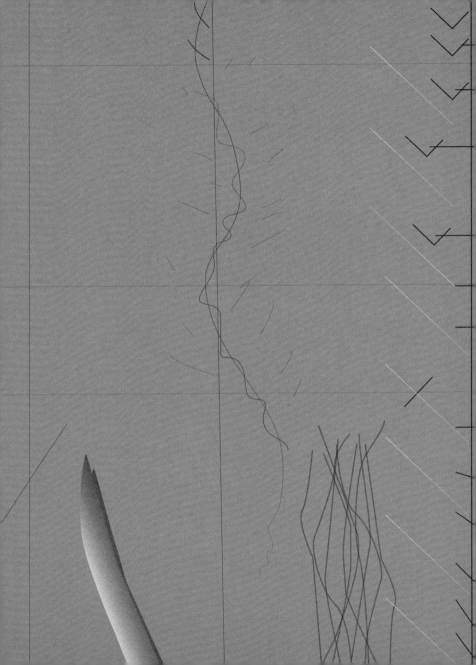

21

ALL THE WEATHER REPORTS
ALL THE HOROSCOPES
ALL THE BIRTHDAY CARDS
THERE WERE NO BIRTHDAY CARDS
ALL THE THERAPIES

DIDN'T KNOW WHAT THIS WOULD FEEL LIKE.

TWO TRUCKS HEADING TOWARDS EACH OTHER
ON A CHICKEN-NECK DRIVEWAY.

NOT A MATH PROBLEM BUT 200 YARDS APART
SQUINTING TO SEE FOR THE FIRST TIME IN
HOW LONG HAS IT BEEN.

MAYBE THEY'LL JUST DRIVE BY
IN AGREEMENT

NOT YET TIRED OF SILENCE.

WHAT DOES BANTAM SEE.
A DUDE IN HIS WAY POSSIBLY AN ASSHOLE.

BANTAM SO LARGE AND DIFFERENT. IF THAT'S HIM.
IT'S HIM OF COURSE IT'S HIM.

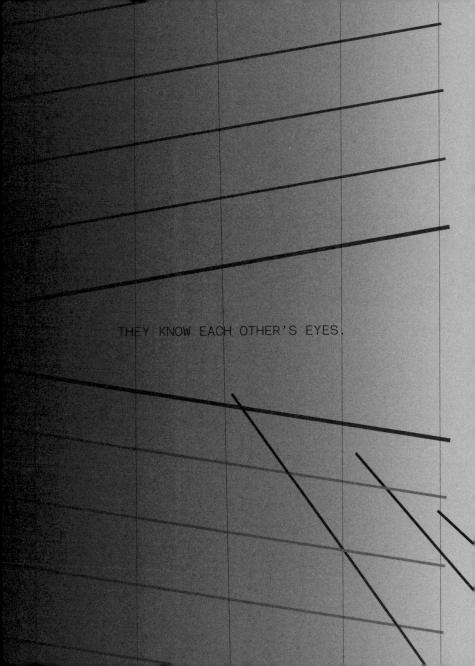

THEY KNOW EACH OTHER'S EYES.

22

HONK HONK

OH MY GOD
IS HE SERIOUS.

NOW THE DOG IS BARKING.

ARE YOU FUCKING KIDDING ME.

THIS SHIT COULD GO DOWN COMPLETELY
THROUGH SOUND EFFECTS.

ONE OF THEM COULD PULL OVER AND LET
THE OTHER ONE PASS.

COULD.

HONK

OR USE THE ENGLISH LANGUAGE.

SLAM

BANTAM GETS OUT.

BARK HOWL MOAN

HIGH WINDS MAKES TO OPEN HIS DOOR
BUT IT'S STUCK. HE GETS IT BUT

BANTAM CATCHES IT.

BOTH THEIR HANDS GRIP THE OPEN DOOR
OF THE NEIGHBOR'S TRUCK.

THIS IS A PRIVATE DRIVEWAY.

SORRY I THOUGHT YOU'D PULL OVER.

WELL IT'S MY DRIVEWAY.

SORRY.

HEY I GOT YOUR POSTCARD.

EXCUSE ME.

AND I ANSWERED YOUR AD.

UM.

BANTAM IT'S ME. HIGH WINDS.

I DON'T KNOW ANYONE
BY THAT NAME.

AND NOW TO VANQUISH

ALL THE ICEBERGS

INSIDE THE PHANTASMAGORIA

CAPTURE THEIR EQUIPMENT

DESTROY THE PASSAGES

AND THANK ALL THE PEOPLE WHO GAVE YOU
THE IDEAS

HOW AM I SUPPOSED TO SAY THANK YOU

THAT'S YOUR PROBLEM ISN'T IT

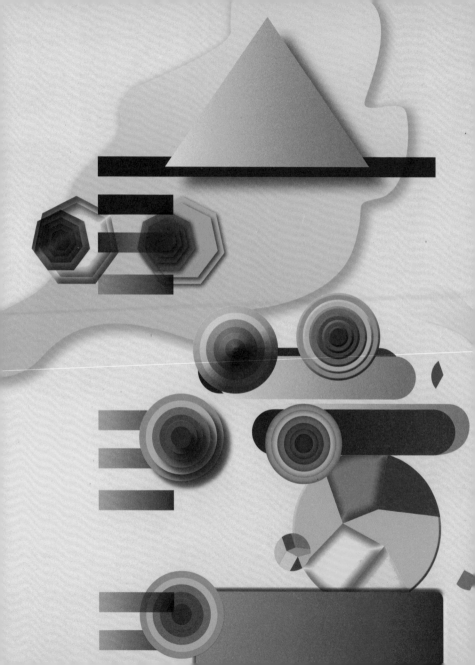

I SAW A COWSKIN RUG BACK THERE

SO I ROLLED IT UP AROUND ME

AND NOW I HAVE THE FORTUNE

THE CHAMBER IS FILLING WITH SMOKE

THE COW LADY HAS A RAY GUN

SHE TRICKED YOU WHEN YOU WENT TO THE
BATHROOM AT NIGHT

SHE JUMPED OUT FROM BEHIND THE CURTAIN

YOU SHOULD ALWAYS CHECK BEHIND THE CURTAIN

ESPECIALLY AT NIGHT

NOW I'LL NEVER HAVE A GIRLFRIEND

WHO SAID ANYTHING ABOUT GIRLFRIENDS
THERE ARE SEVEN MILLION BOYFRIENDS AN ARMY

SO WHAT

THE BOYFRIENDS HAVE THE GIRLFRIENDS OUTNUMBERED

WELL THE GIRLFRIENDS HAVE TACTICAL BRILLIANCE
THEY WILL ALWAYS SURVIVE
WHAT DO YOU SAY TO THAT

THE BOYFRIENDS HAVE WEAPONS

SO DO THE GIRLFRIENDS OF COURSE THEY HAVE WEAPONS
ARE YOU INSANE
THEY MAKE THE WEAPONS
AND THEY GRILL THE HAMBURGERS

THAT IS A NEW LOW EVEN FOR YOU

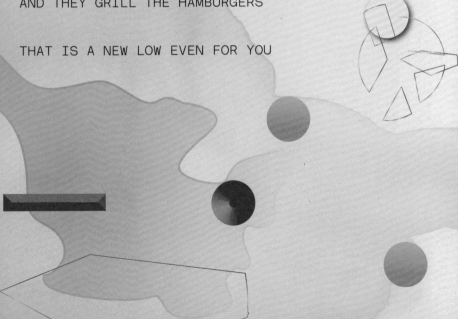

THEY CONTROL TELEVISION
WHO GETS TO WATCH IT
WHO GETS TO BE ON IT
WHO GETS TO EAT DINNER IN FRONT OF IT

THAT IS PURE PHANTASMAGORIA

NO IT'S TUNNEL OF REAL TRUTH EQUATION

THAT SHOW GOT CANCELED BEFORE YOU WERE BORN

I WATCHED RERUNS

YOU WATCHED PERMISSION PLEASE MISTRESS

WHO CARES

YOU WATCHED CUTE PEOPLE TIME

STOP OR I'LL BLANCHE YOU

YOU WATCHED ALL THE WORST THINGS THE THINGS
THAT NOBODY SHOULD WATCH AND YOU WERE ALLOWED
TO THAT IS THE MOST OFFENSIVE PART

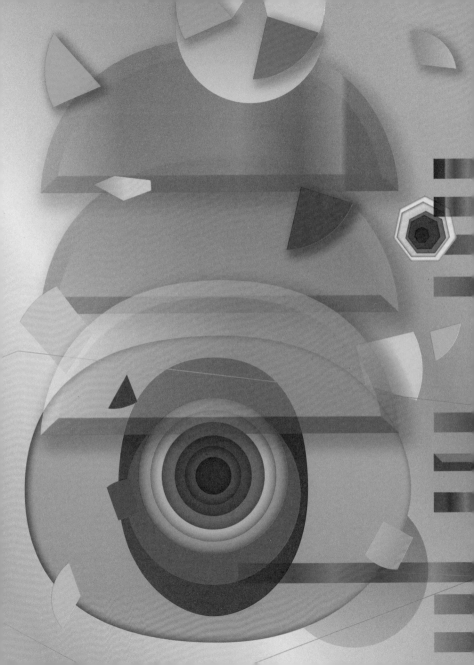

I CAN'T HELP IT IF I WAS
ALLOWED
COME ON YOU LOSER THE PORTAL
IS HERNIATING QUICKLY

IS THAT WHY YOU HATE ME

HERE, A STALLION

WHAT

HERE, THROW YOURSELF
THIS IS THE FINAL BEACON

25

HIGH WINDS DISAVOWS ALL OF THOSE WHITE MEN.

THEIR PANORAMA FANTASY.

SWEEPING COMIC BOOK TRUE WAR ADVENTURES

INNER HARMONY (DOMINATION) QUEST THROUGH
THE BLANK PAGE.[3]

WHICH WE ALL KNOW WAS NEVER BLANK JUST
ILLEGIBLE TO THEM.

OR THEY WERE BLINDED BY THEIR OWN DARKNESS.
A GREAT MANY STILL ARE.

WHICH IS NO EXCUSE.

THERE ARE NO EXCUSES.

NOT FOR HIM EITHER.
PUNISHES SELF ALL THE WAY HOME.

YOU NEED TO HOPE
THAT SOMEONE IS NICER THAN YOU ARE

BECAUSE YOU'RE NOT NICE ALL THE TIME.

YOU'RE NOT MEAN BUT IT'S MORE LIKE YOU JUST
ACT ON IMPULSE AND YOUR IMPULSE IS TO TAKE
WHAT YOU WANT AND NOT PUT OTHER PEOPLE FIRST.
SINCE NO ONE BLUDGEONED YOU WITH CONVENTIONS
YOU ALSO DON'T KNOW.
AND YOU DON'T KNOW IF PEOPLE NOTICE.

MAYBE THEY DON'T BECAUSE PEOPLE ARE
CONCERNED WITH THEMSELVES.

SO YOU CAN MAKE UP STORIES

WITH DEMONS IN THEM

ALL

        DAY

                LONG.

AND WHEN YOU'RE LUCKY
BECAUSE SOMEONE IS GENEROUS
IT'S A SURPRISE
AND REMINDS YOU
THAT YOU HAD A CHANCE TO DO
THAT AND YOU DIDN'T.

SO FILL UP THE GAS TANK

A S S H O L E.

ALL THE WAY.

PART FIVE

27

THERE'S NOWHERE TO PARK THIS TRUCK
OFF FAIRFAX.

TAKES A SIESTA IN RITE-AID PARKING LOT

THEN BUYS PLASTIC BAGS.

FOLDS NOTES INTO A SMALL BOOK.

ZIPS BOOK INTO BAG.

DOUBLE-BAGS

TO SAVE FROM OFF CHANCE OF RAIN.

TOSSES IN BACK OF TRUCK FOR NEIGHBOR TO FIND.

HIGH WINDS SWEARS HE ONCE SAID: ANYTIME.

TEXT MESSAGE.

DO YOU HAVE A SEC

WHAT'S UP

NEEDED MY TRUCK YESTERDAY

HIGH WINDS NOT SURE WHAT DAY IT IS.

SORRY I SHOULD HAVE ASKED

RODE MY BIKE GOT SUNBURNT

THOUGHT YOU HAD YOUR OTHER CAR

LOANED IT

HIGH WINDS SURE NEIGHBOR IS ANGRY. BURNS
WITH REMORSE. KEEPS IT CASUAL.

OH SHIT. I O U

HEADS UP WOULD HAVE BEEN NICE

HOW TO APOLOGIZE AND NOT GROVEL. BE SORRY
BUT STRONG.

IT WAS TOO LATE TO TEXT.
WON'T HAPPEN AGAIN.

HIS REASONS NOT PERSUASIVE.

ARE YOU MISSING SOMETHING

???

I FOUND A BAGGIE? WITH... PAPERS IN IT?

THOUGHT HE'D READ IT AND LOVE HIS TRUCK'S CAMEO
BUT GUESS NOT IF HE WAS ANGRY.

UH THAT'S FOR YOU

WHAT IS IT

A BOOK I MADE

NEIGHBOR IS NOT FASCINATED.

COOL

BUY YOU A BEER LATER

MAYBE ANOTHER TIME

JASMINE SEASON BEGINS AND ENDS.

"EVERYONE" IS TIRED OF TALKING ABOUT
LOS ANGELES LIGHT[4]

STILL THE SAME AND UNDRAMATIC

PEOPLE CALL IT INSPIRING OR MADDENING

THE WAY IT FLATTENS THINGS.

"UNHIERARCHICAL." EASY FOR WHO TO SAY.

IF YOU ASK HIGH WINDS

THE SUN JUST SETS

AND TAKES

ALL THE INFORMATION WITH IT.

NOTES ON SOURCES OF INFORMATION

1. *Carlsbad Caverns National Park Service Guidebook*, 1940.

2. Bob Hoff's Carlsbad Caverns History Blog featured an oral history of the holdup as told by a former Caverns employee who chose to remain anonymous. Hoff was a National Parks Service Ranger and Park Historian at Carlsbad Caverns.

3. *The Great Plains* by Walter Prescott Webb first published in 1931.

4. "LA Glows" by Lawrence Weschler from *The New Yorker*'s issue of 2/23/1998 informed this section.

SLEEP AIDS

AMBIEN
ATIVAN
BEDROOM OPTIMIZATION
  GET IT REALLY DARK
  NO ACTIVITY IN BEDROOM EXCEPT SLEEP OR SEX
  NO TECH OR WORK IN BEDROOM
CALIFORNIA POPPY
CANNABIS (INDICA)
CHAMOMILE
DON'T LIE DOWN UNTIL YOU'RE SLEEPY
EAR PLUGS/EYE MASK
EROTIC EXPERIENCE
EXERCISE EARLIER IN THE DAY
HERBAL TEA
HYPNOSIS
MEDITATION
MELATONIN
MUSCLE RELAXERS
PASSIONFLOWER
PROGRESSIVE MUSCLE RELAXATION
READING
SKULLCAP
SLEEP HYGIENE
STOP DRINKING ALCOHOL
STOP DRINKING SO MUCH CAFFEINE
TECHNOLOGY FAST
TRAZODONE
VALERIAN ROOT
WARM MILK
WHITE NOISE MACHINE
WINDING-DOWN RITUALS

(PARTIAL LIST—WE WELCOME YOUR SUGGESTIONS)

ANOTHER PLATEAU
A TIME FOR TESTOSTERONE
BATTLE OF THE BREAKUP
BUTCH RANGER
COWBOYS IN GLASSES
DAY JOB OR DESTINY
DEVIL'S SWIM TRUNKS
DON'T CALL ME LADY
DREAD FOR BREAKFAST
GAY CANYON
THE GOD OF INSOMNIA
GUNS OF WEAKLINGS
HORSE-LIKE LAUGHTER
THE LAST NARRATIVE
LEARNING STICK, OR MANUAL TRANSMISSION
LONE TEACHER
THE MAN WHO CAME FOR DESSERT
NEVER ASK TO STEAL
NO MAN'S COUCH
NOT A LESBIAN ANYMORE
NEUROTIC CROSSFIRE
OVERREACTION TOWN
PARKING LOT SHOWDOWN
PASSING TRICKS
PECTORAL FLY
PHANTOM DICK
PORNOGRAPHY MOUNTAIN
QUEER BUTTE
REALISTIC BULGE
ROTTEN PAYCHECKS (PUBLISHED
AS PAYCHECK MELEE IN EUROPE)
SIDE-EFFECT DRAW
SLEEPING AT THE WRONG TIMES
TEN TALES OF BOREDOM
TRAIL OF BROKEN FRIENDSHIP
TRAUMA RIDERS
TREADMILL HIATUS
UNDER THE ADJUNCT
WHEN EVERYONE'S MARRIED
WHERE WRITERS GO TO DIE
WORRY HARD
THE WRONG WAY
YOU'LL NEVER BIKE TO WORK

FOR CHILDREN
RADICAL BEDTIME SONGS

Writer's Acknowledgments
This book was supported in part by a Faculty Career Development Award
from the Office of the Vice-Chancellor for Equity, Diversity and
Inclusion at UCLA. Revisions to the text were completed at the
Pataphysics Silent Retreat in the Hill Country of Texas in summer 2016
with support from SEG Voices at Select Equity. Early writing took
place at New Dramatists in New York, and an early version of the
material was presented at Enter>Text in Los Angeles.

Thank you to Sue-Ellen Case, Brian Kite, and the UCLA Theater Department
for your support. Thank you Steve Moore for generous feedback on the
text. Love to Marshall Brown, Maria Cataldo, Jordan Harrison, Eric
Hoff, Karinne Keithley, Kristen Kosmas, Sarah Kroll-Rosenbaum and
Michael Wohl, Sawako Nakayasu, Gabriella Reubens, Anna Joy Springer,
Deborah Stein, and Rachel Viola for looking at tiny pictures on my phone
and urging me to continue. Deepest gratitude to my parents and Mo Siedor.

Artist/Designer's Acknowledgments
Thank you first and last to Sylvan Oswald for inviting me on this
beautiful journey; to Dorothy Lin, Jenny Kim, and Vivian Stitzel;
and to Alexandra Grant for enthusiastic support.

Design and production by Jessica Fleischmann / still room
Edited by Florence Grant
Printed by Conti Tipocolor, Florence, Italy
First edition of 1,500
Typeset in Lettera and Bend and printed on Munken Print

Library of Congress Cataloging-in-Publication Data
is available on request.
ISBN 978-0-9988616-0-9

X Artists' Books
PO Box 3424
South Pasadena, CA 91031 USA
www.xartistsbooks.com